SCARY SPOOKY

DHISHA SHREE

Made with ♥ on the Notion Press Platform
www.notionpress.com

I dedicate this book to my mother and my teachers.

Contents

Prologue

This book contains five different horror genre stories.

The first story is about Saara and Lucy. Lucy takes vengeance against her stepmother for her evil character but doesn't hurt Saara and becomes her saviour.

The second story is about problems faced by Beccy and her friends during their adventure trip. How they overcame their problems with the help of their parents and others?

The third story is about Nyra who looks terrified due to her experience in school camp after playing a game. Then her parents gave what type of treatment to get over her fear?

The fourth story is about the Kate celebrating her birthday with her family and friends. At the end of the celebrations, it turns out to be the worst experience for everyone. Finally, how they found the solution?

The last story is about Kayla and her siblings traveling to a cave. How they escaped from that place and who helped them?

I

The Street

An alluring girl named Saara. Saara is a fair, slim, and medium-height girl. She has a round face with small blue eyes. Saara has a pointed nose with short blond hair and rosebud lips. She is a very kind-hearted girl. Saara lives in a city. Her residence is surrounded by many neighboring streets. Saara's house is small but beautiful and surrounded by a dazzling garden with unique plants like viburnum trilobum, coneflower, lobelia, wintergreen, and a few more plants.

Saara's neighboring streets and houses are beautiful like Saara's house but except for one street named "**I WILL DRINK YOUR BLOOD**". On this street, there is only one house. The house is so old and broken down. The blood is split over on some parts of the house and more spider webs with worms.

Every day Saara jogs in her neighboring streets. One day unknowingly, she was jogging in "**I WILL DRINK YOUR BLOOD**" street. Suddenly Saara heard a sound and it said: "**I WILL KILL YOU**". Saara couldn't understand where the sound came from and why it said that. Again and again, the sound came and it said "**I WILL KILL YOU**", "**I WILL KILL YOU**", "**I WILL KILL YOU**",

"**I WILL KILL YOU........**", then Saara stopped jogging. She slowly walked near the old and broken-down house. Saara screamed because she saw a **phantom** full of blood, and dirt. It has an **aperture** between all parts of the body. After seeing this Saara fainted. After some time Saara awaken and went back home.

The next day Saara once again went to the street and saw the street name was "**I WILL DRINK YOUR BLOOD**". Then Saara remembered that once her neighbour said not to jog in that street because they came to know that the street had a haunted house with aphantom so, Saara's neighbour said her not to go by that street. Even though Saara went to the street and went into the haunted house and she was a little scared. Saara saw many skeletons with blood and dirt. After seeing this Saara saw a room and she went into the room. Saara saw a **marionette**. It is not just a marionette it is a phantom named **Lucy**.

A few years before, Lucy's father married Lauren to take care of his daughter Lucy after her mother's death. But she doesn't like Lucy. She tortured Lucy in absence of her father. Lauren pretends before her husband that she loves Lucy. Lucy was killed by her stepmother Lauren without the knowledge of Lucy's father. Then Lucy became a spirit. Lucy was very angry and tried to kill her stepmother, Lauren. Then Lauren called a ghost hunter. The ghost hunter locked the ghost in one of the rooms in that old house, and Lucy was waiting to take revenge against her stepmother.

Later Saara went into the haunted house and Lucy tried to kill Saara because she is Lauren's daughter. Lucy touched Saara and fell out of the room because she was wearing a divine locket. Saara asked Lucy **"WHO ARE YOU**?" with a terrified look on her face.

Lucy said to Saara, "I am your half-sister" and was killed by her mother Lauren. And also explained how was she tortured and killed by *her stepmother. After Saara knew about her mother's vicious mind, she became furious. Seeing the reaction of Saara's anger in her eyes against her mother, Lucy changed her thought about killing Saara. Lucy said that* **"I WILL KILL LAUREN ONE DAY"** *and disappeared all of a sudden.*

Saara's mother Lauren was waiting in the house for a long time and she went in search of Saara. Finally, she came to the old haunted house and heard the conversation between Saara and Lucy. After returning to the house, she kept Saara under her custody in a room. Saara didn't stop, she tried to tell the truth to others about Lucy's murder but her efforts went in vain. Lauren came to know about Saara's ideas. She started to frighten and torture Saara. To save Saara from her mother, Lucy appeared before Saara and Lauren. Lucy killed her stepmother with her special powers. Then she handed over Saara safely to her father to take care of by revealing the truth to him. Lucy's soul became Saara's bodyguard. That haunted street and house became normal. If anyone tries to hurt Saara, Lucy appears as her saviour.

II

Beccy and her friendson the trail

There were four friends named Beccy, Victoria, Charlotte, and Nadia. They lived in Orlando, located in Florida. Every six months they go to the theme park twice. So, they met each other in the Paradise theme park on Friday this time. They love to play all rides in the amusement park. There were two coaster rides. The first was Mr. Freeze and the second was Intimidator. They all enjoyed both rides which were their favourite. Then they went to water rides and snow kingdom.

After returning from the amusement park, Beccy asked her friends "Let all of us go trekking to Ocala Forest in Florida". Victoria and Charlotte were very happy but Naida was afraid of animals and darkness in the forest.

Beccy said Naida not to be afraid, "we all will have great experience and enjoyment". Then they decided to go trekking by next week.

Beccy and her friends started their trekking one fine morning with a lot of happiness and expectation. While trekking they saw various trees such as Sand live oak, Scrub palm, silver maple, Slash pine, and some birds like the Roseate spoonbill, Black skimmer, Wood stork, and many more trees and birds. They walked a long way and it was almost evening. Victoria was tired so everybody decided to take a rest.

They saw a river nearby and they went near the river to view a beautiful sunset. Now it's dark in the forest, so Charlotte said we can put our tent here tonight for sleep. Beccy brought wood and lightened them by fire. They started to cook dinner with vegetables brought by them. They had their delicious dinner. Now they went inside the tent.

After sometimes Nadia heard some **strange & anomalous sounds**. She got frightened. Her friends soothed her and made her take a rest. Now it's almost midnight everybody slept. Victoria woke up around 4.30 a.m. and came out of the tent. She saw a **weird apparition** walking towards their tent. She became petrified, and *nervous, and started to scream. Then Charlotte, Beccy, and Nadia came out of the tent and asked What happened?*

*Victoria showed that weird apparition to her friends also. but when they turned to see, it came near to their face and disappeared. Everybody was **panic-stricken** and they decided to move from that place immediately. While returning from the forest, they saw an old man. He asked them " Who are you all? and What are you all doing here?" They explained to him about their trekking and night stay near the river. He was shocked and asked, **"What near the river?"** Yes, **"Why are you shocked?"** He said to them, in this forest during night time many unusual sounds and abnormally someone roaming near the river. Many of them were affected by these strange incidents. He asked them to leave the forest immediately. Finally, they came out of the forest and went to Beccy's house.*

When reaching Beccy's house, it was almost night so they decided to stay there tonight. They all slept in Beccy's room. The next morning, Nadia, Victoria, and Charlotte went to their houses. After a day Beccy heard strange sounds in her house. She was frightened and called her friends to tell them about her experience last night. Beccy made a conference call to her friends, everyone said they also heard the same sound last night in their room. After ending the phone call, they all realized that all four of them are in the same place where they stayed in the forest.

Victoria and Nadia were terrified but Beccy and Charlotte said not to be scared. They said, **"We all should hold our hands tightly and never leave in any situation"**. They started to walk from that place and they were hearing strange sounds around them. They again met the old man and explained their situation. They asked him to help them get rid of this problem. The old man said that only one person can save them from this problem. You all go and meet the holy person in the deep forest and showed them the way to go there. They came across many hurdles and problems. Finally, they reached the holy person's place.

They met the holy person and explained everything in detail. They also asked him," **Who is the ghost? and why it is following us?"** The holy person spoke to that ghost. After speaking the holy person said that "The ghost is your neighbour Natalie who died last year ". She thinks that the reason for her death is Beccy and her friends.

They all were shocked when Natalie appeared before them. With full anger, Natalie shouted, " I won't reprieve you all". Then four friends pleaded with Natalie and explained to her that they aren't the reason for her death. Beccy got up from her bed with diaphoresis on her face. She was in deep shock and couldn't answer the questions asked by her friends. After some time, Beccy realized that it was just a dream. Then she saw the time, it was early morning. She was in confusion about whether her dream will happen in reality or not with fear.......

III

End Game???

One day Nyra looks very terrified and her family members asked her "Why are you always looking tensed and terrified". Nyra said no, I am feeling and looking normal but her mom saw her reaction and asked what happened again and again. Nyra said in her school camp, she faced a horrendous incident. She started to explain her experience in the camp.

Last week we had five days camp on our school campus. All students are asked to assemble on the school ground before 8.30 a.m. We are asked to stand in groups according to our team allotment list. Each group consists of three seniors and two juniors. The seniors are given instructions to take care of juniors on their team. On the first day, we started with the school prayer. After the prayer, we had an introduction session for all the students. In this session, we have to self-introduce ourselves. Then we all had our mid-break for 15 mins and asked to assemble again near the stage. We had interesting sessions till lunch. After a one-hour lunch break, we continued our sessions again till evening 6. pm. We had our dinner at 7 p.m. and then at 8'o clock, we all assembled for fire camp till 9.30 p.m. In the fire camp, we had singing, and dancing performances and also played games. Finally, we went to sleep at night by 10 p.m.

The next day we had the same routine with some interesting sessions on how to help others in the time of emergency, self-defense classes, etc... After going to bed my seniors Karishma, Taara and Avni were awake and were discussing something and after some time I was asleep. It was nearly 2:15 am and my seniors woke me and my friend, Mansi, and told us to sit beside them as they were going to play a horror game **"Ghost Paper Challenge."**

My seniors first gathered all the necessary supplies needed to play. We had a piece of paper, a pen, a candle,and a match, and we played near our room door. We were preparing to play by turning off all the lights in our room. We placed a piece of paper on the floor in front of *the closed door, lit a candle, and placed it next to the paper. We waited until* **3 a.m.** *When the clock hits 3, we knocked three times on the door and repeated:* **"spirit of the door, I welcome you; make yourself present and come through."** *We started to communicate. We used our pens to write down a question on the paper. Then placed the pen on the paper and slide them both halfway under the door. We waited for the reply.*

If the paper does not move or does not receive the paperback, we should then skip to the last step to end the game. If successful, we may repeat this until we asked three questions. We should then end the game. To do so, we should **thank the spirit, and blow out our candle.** *We should also make sure to keep the* **door shut until the sun rises and daylight is present.**

After we finished playing the game, my senior Taara opened the door. We saw something standing outside our room. She quickly shut the door and came to bed. But till the morning we heard some weird sounds and felt someone tapping the door very hard. On the next third and fourth days, during the daytime, we all attended the training but during the night we went and slept early. Around 3.00 a.m. we all heard strange sounds and experienced someone calling us to come out of the room. In fear, we didn't go out of the room on the third day. On *the fourth day, we opened the door to face it. It started to attack us. We left that place and ran to get help from others. We shouted, "**Somebody helps us but no one heard our voice**". We went to the divine room in our camp and returned to our room in the morning. Finally, fifth day evening we all returned to our houses.*

After returning from camp, till now I'm hearing those strange sounds, someone standing in front of me and calling me to come out of the house during the night. I'm feeling terrified and don't know how to get rid of this problem. Mom, please help me to end this game and to come out of this complicated issue. Mom asked Nyra, "Did you speak with your teammates, what is their situation?" Nyra replied, "No, I didn't speak with any of my teammates." Mom scolded Nyra and asked her don't panic. Our family will guard you to overcome this situation, don't worry about this issue.

She called her teammates and asked about their experience after returning from camp. They all replied that they had the same experience. Her friend Mansi alone talked about the issue with her family. Then Nyra and Mansi's parents spoke to other teammates' parents.

Parents decided to take them to a psychiatrist to get suggestions about their children's fear. They went to a psychiatrist Ira and explained the issue. first, she explained to them that fear of ghosts is called Phasmophobia. Then She started treatment "Cognitive Talk Therapy", this treatment helps them to understand the root cause of their fear and learn to change their thoughts and beliefs against the fear. and another treatment suggested by her is religious counselling. It may be best to seek counselling with a religious leader in addition to the previous treatment. This will give them the confidence to get rid of the fear. She also suggested that parents not leave their children alone or in dark places for a few days. Always one of the family members to accompany them and have at least a night lamp in each room during the night.

At last, children got rid of the fear after their treatment. Their parents strictly said their children not to repeat this. "Don't play such games which affect your mind, always play some useful and creative games which help you to develop your skills."

IV

Kate's Birthday

On a magnificent day, preparations for Kate's birthday celebration were going on. Already She invited her friends Mackenzie, Rebecca, Evelyn, and Brooklyn to come to the house on her birthday. They all came to her house in the morning to spend time with Kate and make her birthday special. They planned to give a surprise to Kate. They cooked her favourite dishes and baked a surprise birthday cake. They showered her with gifts, and cards and helped Kate's parents Amanda and Patrick to decorate for the birthday bash. Now Preparations were ready to celebrate the birthday. Guests for the birthday started to arrive at the venue. They invited all their business colleagues. All were enjoying the party by dancing, singing, and playing games. It's time Kate cut her birthday cake prepared by her friends. Then all had their dinner and left the party.

All were sitting in the garden and unwrapping the gifts on the table. Suddenly they heard some strange sound coming from inside the house. All turned towards the house with confusion from "where this sound was coming from?" Then some gifts fell so Brooklyn turned towards the table and she noticed Kate was missing. Her friends said to her parents not to worry, they will search for Kate. But Evelyn said she will accompany Kate's parents because they were nervous. She would take care of them and ask others to search for Kate.

Rebecca, Brooklyn, and Mackenzie went and stepped inside the house. It was too dark so they tried to switch on the lights in the house. They could not on even a single light. Then Brooklyn said, let's switch on the torch in their mobile. They held their hands tightly and started to search for Kate. But they realized that they were coming again and again to the living room. In fear, they ran out of the house and came back to the garden. Kate's parents asked them, "What happened, what was that sound, and Where is Kate?", "Why she didn't come with you all?", "What happened to Kate?" Rebecca explained in detail to Kate's parents. They couldn't find Kate.

Kate's parents and her friends went again inside the house. Kate's mother took the cross hanging on the wall of the living room. Now they could go to the other rooms. They found Kate unconscious in her bedroom. Kate's friends lifted her and brought her outside the house. They were trying to wake her. At that time someone gave her water to sprinkle on her face. Mackenzie turned to thank that person and she was shocked. Because the person was none other, it was Kate. She asked Kate " you?" then "Whom we brought out?" Hearing Mackenzie's conversation, others also turned and they were also shocked to see two Kate. Amanda kept the cross in the hands of fainted Kate and she gained consciousness. Then she went near another Kate, and suddenly that Kate disappeared from there. After praying, all went to their rooms to sleep.

The next day, Amanda was thinking about yesterday's incident while cooking in the kitchen. After having breakfast, she decided to consult a holy person about the issue. Amanda and Patrick went to meet the holy person and explained the incident that happened in their house. The holy person said: " there are two ghosts with them and I couldn't find who is doing this." He gave some holy water to them. He said that Kate and her friends should drink this water.

After returning home, Kate's parents called other friends' parents to their house. They told them about the issue and the water given by the holy person to drink. Amanda asked Kate and her friends to drink the water

Then Amanda and Patrick said to Kate's friend's parents that after eating lunch they could go to their homes as it was noon. Kate's friend's parents helped Amanda to make lunch. Then Brooklyn, Rebecca, Mackenzie, Kate, and Evelyn went to Kate's room, and Kate and Rebecca were thirsty, so Kate took her water bottle, but it was empty, so Kate said she was going to fill her bottle, and Evelyn said she would fill the bottle.

Kate's parents are business partners and have some rivals in their business field. Rebecca suddenly came out from Kate's for a walk and saw Evelyn mixing toxins in the water bottle. She was getting puzzled about Evelyn's actions. Evelyn then filled the water bottle and was going to return to the room. Before she entered, Rebecca entered the room and told Kate that Evelyn was mixing toxins in the water bottle. Everyone was shocked and suspected Evelyn's actions for the past few days. When Evelyn brought the bottle, Kate did not drink it and threw the bottle away.

Here the secret is revealed, the rivals of Kate's parents had sent Evelyn and a holy person to kill her family. The Holy person did not mix the toxins as someone arrived, so he gave the poison to Evelyn and told her to blend them into Kate's family's food or drink. Even the things which happened on her birthday were illusions created by mixing chemicals in their food. Kate came to know the truth from Evelyn and told her parents. Her parents complained to the cops then the holy person, Evelyn, and their rivals were arrested.

Dukun Cave

Kayla wakes her siblings up for school one morning. Kayla has two sisters and three brothers named Linda, Hazel, Liam, Julian, and Thiago. The family lives in a beautiful palace in the center of the city. It is surrounded by a lake and has a playground in its garden. It has a water fountain, trees, a flower bed, a playground with a slide, a swing, a trampoline, and a swimming pool.

Due to an accident, their parents died, and since that time Kayla has had to take care of her siblings. After their parents‘ deaths, the money they saved for their kids was given to Kayla. After that, the family was so rich, as they got their parents' money and Kayla was also earning money.

Kayla's siblings were getting ready for school, and they went to school. The next day, their summer holidays were starting. When they came back home, Liam and Hazel started to plan their vacation. Hazel researched paranormal activities, and she found a hysterical ghost cave called "THE DUKUN CAVE." She discussed this with her siblings, and they decided to go to this cave for their vacation.

Linda and Julian are the eldest, and the other three—Hazel, Liam, and Thiago—wanted Julian and Linda to request their elder sister Kayla go to the cave. Kayla didn't believe in the paranormal but agreed to go there anyway. All her five brothers and sisters started to pack everything for their trip to the DUKUN CAVE, like snacks, beverages, and water bottles.

The next day, they took their car to go to the Dukun Cave. They were enjoying the trip by chatting, eating, and playing with their phones and toys.

Even though they were enjoying the trip, at one point they had to change their path by traveling through a hysterical village. When they entered the village, they were shocked to see a taco truck that didn't have any driver to drive it; it was driven by itself. They even saw two dead bodies along the roadside. Somehow, a few people were living there, but they were witches. They were really scared to drive into the village, but they overcame their fear and came out of the village. After coming out of the village, they were traveling through a dense forest. While traveling, they saw a huge tree hollow, and they thought that was the mystical ghost cave, "THE DUKUN CAVE." They parked the car and went inside, but they didn't feel any negative vibrations or anything scary, so they went deep inside the tree hollow and saw another hollow; then everyone realized that the tree hollow they had travelled in was not the Dukun Cave, and the hollow they were now seeing was.

Only a few people have reached the dukun cave, and many others have only reached the tree hollow and not the real cave. Even though they were happy, they didn't reach the end of the cave. Kayla said this was enough, and we can return to our car as we have a long journey to go to our home. The kids agreed with it, but before leaving, they took some pictures of the Dukun Cave.

They came out of the cave and drove their car through the hysterical village. At last, they came home. They were all so tired that they went to sleep. When they awoke the next morning, everyone realized Thiago was missing; they all became tense and went in search of him. They were searching for him the whole day. It was nearly 7 p.m., and they heard some knocking in the basement of their house. Everyone went to the basement and saw Thiago in a glass coffin. They tried to break it, but they could not. He was suffering because he was not able to breathe. Suddenly the coffin broke into pieces, and Thiago was saved by his siblings, but they doubted who knocked on the basement door and who screamed. It was their mother's soul that helped them. Her soul said that while they were traveling, they had disturbed something. But this was not the end; when they tried to get out of the basement room, it was locked, and a demon was inside the room. They were trying to escape, but they couldn't. The demon threw them against the walls with its powers and tried to kill them with its huge fingernails and poisonous hands. If the demon touches a person, they will be turned into ashes.

Suddenly, Kayla had some flashes and remembered that her family has a black magic background and all her siblings had those flashes. At last, all of them had a flash of some words. All Kayla's siblings spelled the words at the same time, which turned into a superpower and blasted the demon.

At last, their parent's souls were living peacefully in the heavens, and their children were living peacefully on earth.